Written by Moira Butterfield

Illustrated by Rosalind Beardshaw

Designed by Lisa Sturley

This edition published by Parragon in 2010
Parragon
Queen Street House
4 Queen Street
Bath BA1 1HE, UK

ISBN 978-1-4054-9435-9

Printed in China

Smile baby smile

PaRragon

Bath · New York · Singapore · Hong Kong · Cologne · Delhi · Melbourne

The sun shone.
The birds flew.
The flowers grew.

But the baby...

The sister tried singing.

The brother tried swinging.

The mommy said "**Coo.**"

The daddy said **"Boo!"**

But the baby...

cried!

The sister played some pit-a-pat.

The brother wore a funny hat.

The mommy made
a shiny star.

The daddy drove around in the car.

But the baby...

The sister kissed
the baby's toes.

The brother kissed
the baby's nose.

The mommy hugged the baby tight.

The daddy kissed them
all good night.

Then the baby did a funny **burp**....

burp

...and then the baby...

...smiled!